おまつりのうた
Impressions of Festivals

日航財団＝編
Edited by The JAL Foundation

ブロンズ新社
Bronze Publishing

『ハイクを世界の子どもたちに』

日本大会審査委員長、俳人　中村 忠男

戦後間もない頃、皇太子殿下の家庭教師だったR・H・ブライスが『HAIKU』の第一巻を著して海外に俳句普及の礎を築いてから六〇年あまり。今や俳句は「ハイク」として海外によく知られるようになりました。多くの国でハイク協会が作られ、俳誌が出版されています。二〇〇九年にベルギーの首相からEUの理事会議長に就任したファンロンパイ氏（EU初代大統領）もハイクを趣味とし、自身のウェブサイトに句を掲載しています。

一九六四年の東京オリンピックの年に米国で実施された日本航空による「ハイクコンテスト」は大きな反響を得て、これをきっかけに豪州やカナダ、英国などでコンテストが行われました。一九九〇年に日航財団が設立されて以降、世界の子どもたちによるハイク大会が二年ごとに実施され、今日に至っています。今回はその十二回目で、テーマは「お祭り」。世界二十五の地域から一万二千句あまりが寄せられました。松尾芭蕉は「俳諧（かい）は三尺（さんせき）の童（わらべ）にさせよ」「子どもの遊ぶごとくせよ」と語ったそうですが、まさにその言葉にぴったりの句がありました。

ギョウザがだんごをご招待
温泉の鍋に飛び込んで
熱くておなかを空に向けたよ

　餃子邀汤圆　跳进锅里泡温泉　热得肚朝天
（Yueming Xu　七歳　中国／上海）

次の句は、少し大人の感性で秋の雰囲気を詠んでいます。

金色のくちびる　言葉飛び交う　秋
Golden lips　Words flying　Autumn
（Lara Ana Kulenović　十一歳　クロアチア）

俳句は作者と読者のあいだの相互作用であり、大人の俳句では共通の体験や感性がないと理解しあえないことが多いのですが、子どもの俳句は、たとえ言語が違ってもわからないということはありません。誰もが、子どもを経験して大人になるわけですから。

戦前に日本に来て、戦時中は収容所に抑留されていたブライスは、終戦まもなく「日本人がもっと俳句を愛していたならば……」と口にしたそうですが、自然と人間への共感に満ちた、豊かな心を育てるハイクを世界に広めたいものです。今回、コンテストに参加した世界の子どもたちが心豊かな大人になって、自分の子どもたちにハイクを教えてくれる日が来てくれることを願っています。

おひなさま　わたしもいっしょに　すわらせて
（仁木円香　七歳）

かかしはね　田んぼのこめと　おどってる
（松嶋朱理　八歳）

*「ハイク」：日本語の五七五で詠まれる「俳句」に対し、海外の母国語で詠まれる三行の詩を「ハイク」と表現しています。外国語で書かれた句は三行ですので、日本語の俳句と比べてさらに多くの言葉が使用できます。

はじめに

Prologue

"Haiku for World Children"

Tadao Nakamura
Chairman of the screening committee for the 12th World Children's Haiku Contest, haiku poet

Some sixty years ago, soon after the end of World War II, Reginald Horace Blyth, who served as a private tutor to the then Crown Prince Akihito, published the first volume of his book, "HAIKU." This influential book helped lay the foundation for recognition and expansion of haiku overseas. Today, this originally indigenous form of poetry has gained worldwide recognition, to the extent that the word "haiku" is listed in the dictionaries of languages around the world. There are haiku societies established and haiku journals published in many countries and regions. Mr. Herman Van Rompuy, former Belgian Prime Minister who in 2009 became the first president of the European Council (often referred to unofficially as president of the European Union), is a haiku poet who posts his works on his personal website.

In 1964, the year of Tokyo Olympic Games, Japan Airlines sponsored a haiku contest in the United States, which drew a significant response. The contest was expanded to cover Australia, Canada and the United Kingdom. Since its establishment in 1990, the JAL Foundation has been hosting the World Children's Haiku Contest every two years. The 12th contest was held during 2011–2012, with participants from 25 countries and regions of the world submitting more than 12,000 haiku composed under the theme of "Festivals".

Matsuo Basho once said, "Let the three-foot-tall child (in yourself) compose haiku" and "Make haiku as children play." Many of the submissions embodied this idea of Basho. To share just a few:

The Doll Festival
Let me sit down
With you all
Madoka Niki, Age 7, Female, Japan

Scarecrows
Dancing with rice ears
In the rice fields
Akari Matsushima, Age 8, Female, Japan

Since haiku composed in foreign languages are in three lines, more words can be used, as in the following haiku:

A fried dumpling inviting a doughboy
They jump in the pot of the hot spring
So hot that they turn their bellies to the sky
Yueming Xu, Age 7, Female, Shanghai, China

The next haiku is the work of an eleven-year-old Croatian girl who expresses an autumn atmosphere with a slightly more mature sensitivity:

Golden lips
Words flying
Autumn
Lara Ana Kulenović, Age 11, Female, Croatia

Since haiku is an interaction between the composer and the reader, haiku composed by adults is sometimes difficult to understand without common experiences or sensitivities. On the other hand, haiku composed by children can be more readily understood regardless of the language in which it is originally composed. Let's face it; we all go through childhood before becoming adults.

R. H. Blyth came to Japan before the war and was interned in a camp during the war. Soon after the war ended and he was released, he often said, "If only the Japanese people had loved haiku a little more." Indeed, haiku helps to nurture a rich spirit that is full of empathy for nature and fellow human beings, and that is why we hope more and more people worldwide will enjoy haiku. It is my wish that the children who participated in the current haiku contest will one day grow into spiritually rich men and women and will pass on the joy of haiku to their children.

1章 おまつりがはじまるよ
Festival Is Starting!

森のお祭り
木は踊(おど)りながら
風と遊んでいるよ

Forest festival
Trees dancing also
Playing with the wind

C'est la fête dans la forêt
Les arbres dansent
Amusés par le vent

Inès Hersan
age 9　Female　Morocco（モロッコ）

夜空にまたたく星
打ち上げの音に驚(おどろ)いて
花火になった

Twinkling stars at night
Surprised by the spurting sounds
Joined in the flowers

■■■■■

Christine Littrice
age12　Female
USA（米国本土）

わくわくどきどき
もうすぐ花火がはじまるぞ
バーン！そら、はじまった！

The anticipation is warming up
The fireworks are about to start
Bang! There they Go!

■ ■ ■ ■ ■

Alex Gibbs
age11　Male
UK（英国）

花がさく
さくらんぼのような真っ赤なかざりつけ
何のお祭り？

Blossom all the plants
Cherry red things are hanging
What festival comes?

▪ ▪ ▪ ▪ ▪

Xing Yuan Tan
age 7　Female
Singapore（シンガポール）

爆(ばく)竹(ちく)に
龍(りゅう)舞(ま)い獅(し)子(し)舞(ま)い
神(か)轎(ご)がゆく

Firecrackers
Dragon dancing and lion dancing
Palanquin moving

神轎繞村莊
舞龍舞獅鑼鼓揚
爆竹鎮日響

Wen-Shin Lu
age11　Female
Taiwan（台湾／台北）

炸裂する色
街のあちこちで競争心
お祭り気分

Exploding colors
Rivalry lurks in the streets
Carnival feeling

■ ■ ■ ■ ■

Noah Hirashima
age14　Male
USA（米国／ハワイ）

Lights and grand parade
Listen to the ringing bell
Viva! It's feast day

Ilaw't parada
Pakinggan ang kampana
Viva! Pista na!

■ ■ ■ ■ ■

Andrea Louise Matulac
age14　Female
Philippines（フィリピン）

光と華々しいパレード
鳴りひびく鐘(かね)をきく
ばんざい！今日はお祭りだ

With the fireworks
Shooting up
Smiling faces bloom

■ ■ ■ ■ ■

品川 瑞華
Mizuka Shinagawa
age10　Female
Japan（日本）

打ちあがる
花火につられて
笑顔さく

Colorful feast day
The happiness it will bring
Nothing can compare

Pistang makulay
Ang kasiyahang taglay
Walang kapantay

■ ■ ■ ■ ■

Shanaia Jane Bual
age12　Female
Philippines（フィリピン）

色があふれる祭りの日
何より一番の
幸せな日がやってくる

A million diamonds soaring
Crowds swarming
Holding tight to strings

■ ■ ■ ■ ■

Elli Collins
age 9　Female
Canada（カナダ）

百万のひし形が上がる
みんな一緒に動く
たこ糸をしっかりにぎって

あまい花のかおり
打ちならすイプの音が
ダンスに命をふきこむ

Sweet scent of flowers
And the pounding of Ipus
Bring the dance to life

Zelda Cole
age12　Female
USA.（米国／ハワイ）

Beautiful dancers
With golden headpieces
Fill the streets of Bali

Megan Lauw
age11　Female
USA（米国／ハワイ）

美しいダンサーたち
金色の帽子(ぼうし)をかぶって
バリの通りにあふれる

除夜の鐘を打ちながら
天から辰年がやってくる
窓の外では花火と爆竹

Stroking the watch-night bell
Fireworks and fire crackers outside the window
Year of the dragon coming from heaven

零点钟声响
窗外烟花耀四方
龙年从天降

■ ■ ■ ■ ■

Xuyang Zhu
age 8　Male
China（中国／上海）

わたしは幸運が大好き
ドラゴンがお年玉を食べちゃった
ドラゴンのパワーが好きよ

I love good fortune
The dragon eats my lee see
I love his powers

■ ■ ■ ■ ■

Isabella Joy Teramae
age 6 Female USA（米国／ハワイ）

ギョウザがだんごをご招待
温泉の鍋に飛び込んで
熱くておなかを空に向けたよ

A fried dumpling inviting a doughboy
They jump in the pot of the hot spring
So hot that they turn their bellies to the sky

饺子邀汤圆
跳进锅里泡温泉
热得肚朝天

Yueming Xu
age 7　Female　China（中国／上海）

満開の桜
バラ色のドレスでかろやかに踊る
すてきなお祭り！

Cherry blossoms in bloom
Airily dancing in a rosy dress
Splendid festival!

Cerisers en fleurs
Ta danse en légère robe rose
Illumine nos fêtes !

▪ ▪ ▪ ▪ ▪

Sixtine Demourgues
age15　Female　France（フランス）

Deepavali Nite
Our house is filled with bright lights
Hearts filled with delight

Rytasha Passion Raj
age 9　Female
Singapore（シンガポール）

ディパバリの夜
明るい光に包まれる我が家
心もあたたかくなる

バーンズ記念日楽しいな
カブにポテト、ハギスを食べて
特別な日

I enjoy Burns Day
Have haggis, neeps and tatties
It's special to me

■ ■ ■ ■ ■

Owen Boyle
age10　Male
UK（英国）

Lanterns hanging high reflect the moon
The fireworks sparkle in the night sky
Happy Lantern Festival

燈籠高高掛
月襯蒼穹映煙火
歡度慶元宵

Yu-Chia Hu
age14　Female
Taiwan（台湾／高雄）

高くつったランタンは月に照らされ
花火は夜空にぱっときらめく
元宵節のお祝いだ

20

虹色の空
気球はシューシュー音たてて
魔法の夢みてるみたい

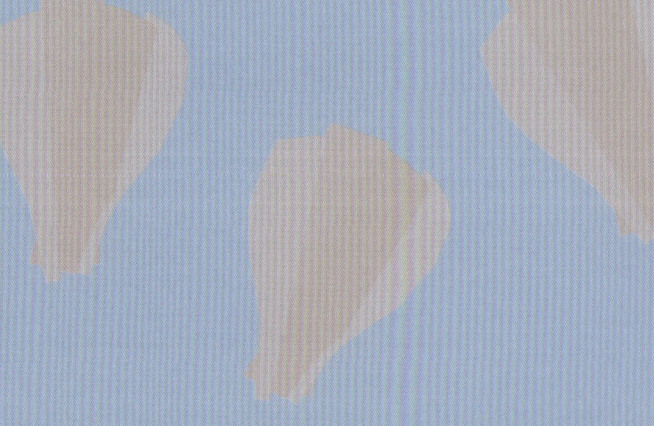

Rainbow-coloured sky
Balloons sizzling outside
Magic dream for our eyes

Ara Magarida Brandao
age11　Female
Portugal（ポルトガル）

Filipino feast
Suckling roast pig is the star
Atop our table

Pinoy ang pista
Kung ang letson ang bida
Sa ating mesa

■ ■ ■ ■ ■

Gabriel Evan Blanco
age14　Male
Philippines（フィリピン）

フィリピンのお祭り
こぶたの丸焼きは主役
テーブル一番のごちそう

十二番目の月の満月の夜に
花の供物(くもつ)を浮かべて願う
来年は洪水がおきませんように

On the night of the full moon in the twelfth month
Floating my krathong and wishing
No floods next year

คืนเพ็ญเดือนสิบสอง
อธิษฐานก่อนลอยกระทง
ปีหน้าน้ำอย่าท่วม

Ornrampha Boonsomchue
age11　Female　Thailand（タイ）

花の提灯ぽつぽつ灯り
子どもたちはなぞなぞに夢中
だれが一番たくさん当てるかな

Lantern of flowers lights up little by little
Children are busy playing riddles
Wondering who will guess most

花灯盏盏亮
小朋友们猜谜忙
比比谁最棒

Yunran Tang
age10　Female
China（中国／上海）

光のお祭り
オレンジや黄色の炎(ほのお)が
夜にゆらめく

Festival of light
Flames of orange and yellow
Flicker in the night

■ ■ ■ ■ ■

Esme Winterbotham
age11　Female
UK（英国）

夜にもえあがる炎(ほのお)
照(て)らしだされる明るさ
真(ま)っ暗闇(くらやみ)を負かす

Fires blazing at night
Illuminated brightness
Dominates the black

■ ■ ■ ■ ■

Robbie Easton
age11　Male
UK（英国）

まつりがみ
結ってこころが
おどり出す

My hair done
For the festival
My heart starts dancing

■ ■ ■ ■ ■

神馬 佳奈美
Kanami Jinba
age10　Female　Japan（日本）

媽(ま)祖(そ)様(さま)は
守り神様
わっしょい、わっしょい！

Goddess Maso is
A guardian deity
Heave-ho, heave, heave-ho!

媽祖來繞境
萬民虔誠迎聖駕
祈國泰民安

■ ■ ■ ■ ■

Jing-Han Liao
age13　Female
Taiwan（台湾／台北）

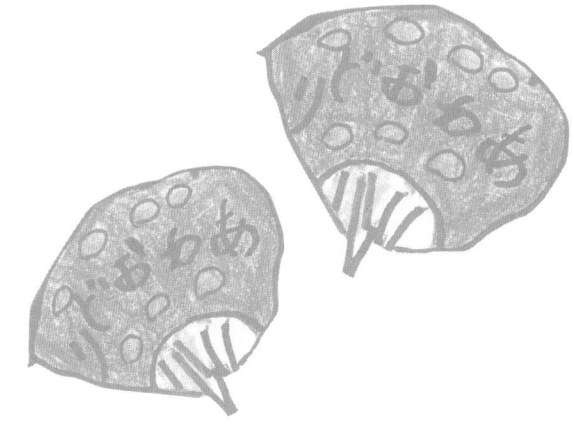

見ているとおどりたくなるあわおどり

Watching
Bon dance in Awa
I feel like dancing, too

安倍　隆之介
Ryunosuke Abe
age 7　Male
Japan（日本）

Today is the 4th
Today is Liberty Day
And it's my birthday

■ ■ ■ ■ ■

Mykola Yashchok
age13　Male
Portugal（ポルトガル）

今日は4日
今日は自由の日
そしてぼくの誕生日(たんじょうび)

In Edinburgh
Bagpipes really, really loud
Lots of drums as well

■ ■ ■ ■ ■

Matthew Burton
age10　Male
UK（英国）

エジンバラの
バグパイプはほんとにほんとに大きな音
たくさんの太鼓(たいこ)もだよ

In the dark town
A rainbow showing up
Bringing happiness

Dans une ville sombre
Je vois un arc-en-ciel
J'apporte la joie

■ ■ ■ ■ ■

Lucie Bellegarde
age 9　Female
Morocco（モロッコ）

暗い町に
虹(にじ)がかかりはじめたよ
よろこびをつれてきたよ

In Happy New Year
We can get some red packets
Fireworks are pretty

Yan Yan Carol Chang
age 9　Female
China（中国／香港）

新年には
お年玉もらえるよ
花火もきれい

The goldfish I scooped
By aiming at them carefully
Now dancing!

ねらい決め
すくった金魚
おどってる

▪ ▪ ▪ ▪ ▪

実延 大二郎
Daijiro Sanenobu
age12　Male
Japan（日本）

Summer festival
The dragon's fire
Blazing up

なつまつり
りゅうのほのおが
もえあがる

▪ ▪ ▪ ▪ ▪

三木 雄貴
Yuki Miki
age 5　Male
Japan（日本）

Drum sounds fill heaven and earth
Dragon boat sails cleaving the waves
Fish awaken surprised

鼓声震天地
龙舟疾驶碧波里
鱼儿被惊起

▪ ▪ ▪ ▪ ▪

Mila Zou
age10　Female
China（中国／上海）

太鼓の音が天地に響きわたり
ドラゴンボートは波を切って進む
魚はびっくりして目をさます

ドラゴンボートレース
しぶきがあがる
鐘(かね)太鼓(たいこ)

Dragon boat race
Splashes going up
Gongs and drums

歡慶五月五
鑼鼓聲陣陣驚天
龍舟向前衝

■ ■ ■ ■ ■

Chia-Yu Hsieh
age12　Female
Taiwan（台湾／台北）

春節が来た
獅子舞をみていたら
ありがたいお菓子をもらったよ

Chinese New Year's here
Amidst the lion dance cheers
Sweet treats we hold dear

■ ■ ■ ■ ■

Wen Siew Shanna Lim
age11　Female
Singapore（シンガポール）

Cultural music
People dancing and laughing
Rows of tasty food

■ ■ ■ ■ ■

Aleah Carino
age12　Female
USA（米国／グアム）

民族音楽
踊(おど)りながら笑う人々
ずらりと並ぶごちそう

Sweet smell of candy
Hear the happy children laugh
Cultures together

■ ■ ■ ■ ■

Sara Tamadon
age12　Female
USA（米国本土）

あまいキャンディのにおい
幸せな子どもたちの笑い声がきこえる
たくさんの文化が集まって

Colourful balloons
Delicious smell of meat
Kids faces light up

■ ■ ■ ■ ■

Talin Harun
age10　Female
Turkey（トルコ）

色とりどりの風船
おいしい肉のにおい
子どもたちの顔がかがやく

クモが夜をはいまわり
ガイコツがすぐにとび出して
今夜は魔女(まじょ)がノックする

Spiders crawling night
Skeletons jumping out right
Witches knock tonight

■ ■ ■ ■ ■

Zhi-Xin Isaiah Lai
age 7　Male
Singapore（シンガポール）

Walking in the crowd
At the festival
Mom's hand is missing

ในงานเทศกาล
ผู้คนเดินไปมาขวักไขว่
มือแม่หลุดไปแล้ว

■ ■ ■ ■ ■

Chetsinee Chaikhun
age15　Female
Thailand（タイ）

人混みの中を歩く
お祭りで
ママの手が離れた

Bursting with colours
Lanterns dancing in the air
Full of happiness

■ ■ ■ ■ ■

Jessica Williams
age11　Female
UK（英国）

いろんな色にはじけて
空に舞う提灯
幸せがいっぱい

Turkey smells everywhere
Pumpkin sweets full of love
Mama will kiss you, baby

火鸡香飘溢
南瓜饼里裹恩情
妈妈亲亲你

■ ■ ■ ■ ■

Xiangheng Chen
age11　Female
China（中国／上海）

どこも七面鳥のにおい
愛情たっぷりカボチャのお菓子
ママのキスがまってるよ

Soybean paste becomes matured
With its sound
Spring is here at last

장이 익는다
너의 소리를 따라
봄이 왔단다

■ ■ ■ ■ ■

Yejin Lee
age13　Female
Korea（韓国）

味噌が熟成する
プクプクという音とともに
春がとうとうやってきた

Loy Krathong this year
Flooded up to our knees
We floated our house instead

ลอยกระทงปีนี้
น้ำท่วมบ้านสูงถึงหัวเข่า
ลอยบ้านแทนกระทง

■ ■ ■ ■ ■

Orathai Yimyoung
age11　Female
Thailand（タイ）

今年のロイ・クラソン祭りは
洪水で膝（ひざ）までの水
かわりにお家を浮かべたよ

War is in the past
We remember those soldiers
Poppy fields are red

■ ■ ■ ■ ■

Sandra Zelic
age12　Female
Australia（オーストラリア）

戦争は過去
兵士たちを思い出す
芥子（けし）の花畑は真っ赤に染まる

Bright lights fill the air
Small lanterns in the heavens
Flickering with hope

■ ■ ■ ■ ■

Simpkins Zena
age14　Female
USA（米国／ハワイ）

明るい光が空気をみたす
空の小さな提灯（ちょうちん）が
希望でちらちら光る

2章 きせつのなかで
In Seasons

クリスマスが来る
プレゼントがとどく
光がかがやいている

Christmas comes
Gifts are coming
Lights are shining

Božič je prišel
Darila prihajajo in
Lučke gorijo

Jan Tunanovič
age10　Male　Slovenia（スロベニア）

レモン祭り
天地の黄金
春を呼ぶ

A festival of lemon
Gold from earth and heaven
Calling spring

■ ■ ■ ■ ■

Mayu Hirata
age10　Female　France（フランス）

Getting Angpow on Chinese New Year
The kids' pockets get bigger
Adults' are empty

ตรุษจีนได้อั่งเปา
ลูกหลานรับเงินกระเป๋าตุง
ผู้ใหญ่กระเป๋าแห้ง

■ ■ ■ ■ ■

Thitirat Saeoung
age11　Female
Thailand（タイ）

春節にもらうお年玉
子どもたちのポケットはふくらんで
大人たちのは空っぽ

Pink cherry blossoms
Falling one by one
Make it a sweet world

분홍 벚꽃잎
하나 둘 떨어지면
달콤한 세상

■ ■ ■ ■ ■

Minju Im
age14　Female
Korea（韓国）

ピンクの桜の花びら
ひとひらずつ散って
美しい世界をつくる

The Doll Festival
Let me sit down
With you all

■ ■ ■ ■ ■

仁木 円香
Madoka Niki
age 7　Female
Japan（日本）

おひなさま
わたしもいっしょに
すわらせて

Ochna and peach are blossoming
The Tet Holiday atmosphere is everywhere
Mr. Sun is smiling

Hoa đào, hoa mai nở
Không khí Tết tưng bừng, rực rỡ
Ông mặt trời mỉm cười

■ ■ ■ ■ ■

Lam Thu Huynh Tran
age11　Female
Vietnam（ベトナム）

梅の花も桃の花もさいて
どこも旧正月の気分にみちている
お日さまが笑っているよ

39

Ding-dong. Who is it?
"Trick or treat", they say laughing
I don't have candies!

Constanca Duarte
age12　Female
Portugal（ポルトガル）

ピンポーン、どなた？
笑いながら「お菓子(かし)くれなきゃいたずらするぞ」って
お菓子(かし)は持っていないわよ！

かわいいピーターコンたち
頭につくりもののご飯の蒸籠(せいろ)
今日はご飯(はん)はないよ

The cute Phitakhons
With disguised sticky rice cooking baskets on their heads
No sticky rice today

ผีตาโขนน่ารัก
หวดน้อยแปลงร่างอยู่บนหัว
วันนี้งดนึ่งข้าว

Chalita Kaeokoon
age11　Female　Thailand（タイ）

サンタクロースはねむりこんで
プレゼントがもらえなかった
だから悲しいんだよ

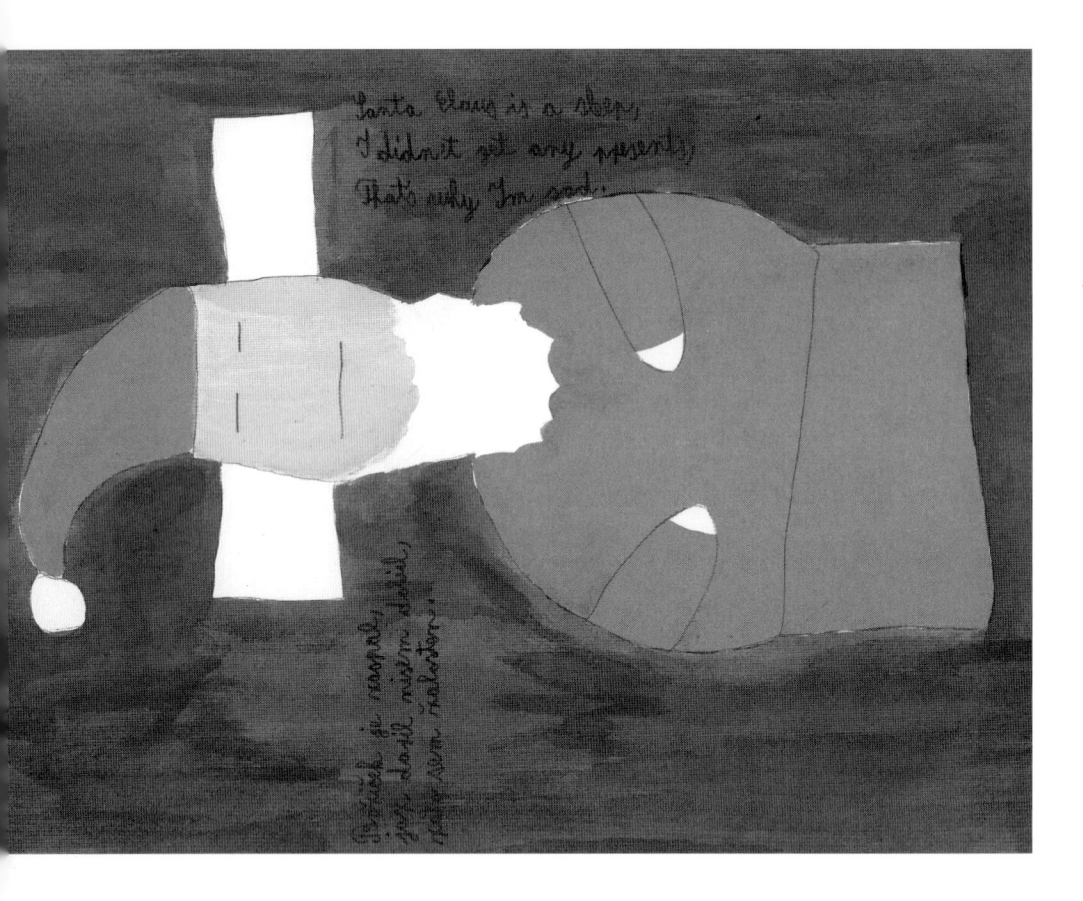

Santa Claus is asleep
I didn't get any presents
That's why I'm sad

Božiček je zaspal
Jaz daril nisem dobil
Zato sem žalosten

Jan Eller
age10　Male　Slovenia（スロベニア）

It is Christmas time
Firecrackers are everywhere
Snow is falling

Božič je prišel
Petarde pokajo
Sneg pada

■ ■ ■ ■ ■

Marko Lumbar
age10　Male
Slovenia（スロベニア）

クリスマスの時が来た
爆竹(ばくちく)があちこちで鳴る
雪(ま)が舞い落ちている

I like Christmas best
Turkey is for my dinner
Presents are all mine

■ ■ ■ ■ ■

Long Yat Chow
age11　Male
China（中国／香港）

クリスマスが大好き
ディナーには七面鳥
プレゼントは全部ぼくのもの

Christmas
Santa surfs
On the wave

■ ■ ■ ■ ■

Lilian Shepherd
age 9　Female
Australia（オーストラリア）

クリスマス
サンタサーフィン
なみの上

もうすぐクリスマス
心の底から
あたたかくやさしい気持ち

Noel coming closer
From the bottom of my heart
Warmth and sweetness

Quand noel approche
Dans nos coeurs
Chaleurs et doucers

Carla Stanichi
age13　Female　France（フランス）

雪だるまをつくってる
夜になってうさぎが
オレンジ色の鼻を食べちゃった

We're making a snowman
At night
The rabbit ate his orange nose

Snežaka delamo
Ponoči mu je zajček
Pojedel nos

Sara Ferlež
age 9   Female
Slovenia（スロベニア）

通りにいるライオン
紙の提灯が
大晦日の夜を照らす

Lions in the street
Paper lanterns light the night
Of the New Year's Eve

■ ■ ■ ■ ■

Ella Pobre
age10　Female
USA（米国／グアム）

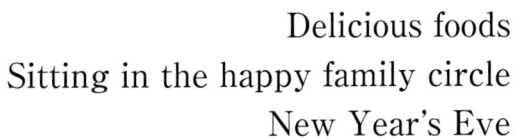

Delicious foods
Sitting in the happy family circle
New Year's Eve

歡喜過新年
全家一起吃團圓
快樂迎新年

■ ■ ■ ■ ■

Chia-Ning Chuang
age13　Female
Taiwan（台湾／台北）

ごちそうと
一家だんらん
大晦日（おおみそか）

お正月がやってきた
みんなで新年のご挨拶
一緒に新しい旅を計画しよう

Chinese New Year comes
We greet each other
Plan for a new journey together

農曆新年到
互相祝賀問句好
共創新旅途

- - - - -

Hei Long Ma
age 7　Male
China（中国／香港）

Firecrackers sound high and low
Lively Dragon dance and Lion dance in the street
Wish everyone a happy new year

鞭炮聲連連
舞龍舞獅好熱鬧
恭賀新喜年

■ ■ ■ ■ ■

Ya-Tze Wu
age12　Female
Taiwan（台灣／高雄）

爆竹は高く低く響き
通りでは元気な獅子舞と龍の舞
みんなに新年おめでとう

Laughters spread around
Little fish looks around
Ooh! Chinese New Year has come!

傳來歡笑聲
小魚兒探頭張望
啊!新春到了!

■ ■ ■ ■ ■

Wan Chun Ashley Wong
age 8　Female
China（中国／香港）

笑い声がひろがる
こざかなが見まわす
おお、春節がきたよ！

A ritual dance with a lion's mask
Reaching the clouds
Spring drums

冬去春到來
鑼鼓鞭炮響雲宵
舞獅迎新年

■ ■ ■ ■ ■

Chin-Ting Hsu
age 7　Female
Taiwan（台湾／台北）

獅子舞の
雲までとどけ
春太鼓

どんぐりが
おつきみしてる
おどりだす

An acorn
Enjoying the moon
And starting to dance

■ ■ ■ ■ ■

村上 華奈映
Kanae Murakami
age 4   Female
Japan（日本）

New Year celebration and Pchum Ben Day
Gathering at the pagoda to do good deeds
Play Khmer popular games

ចូលឆ្នាំបុណ្យភ្ជុំបិណ្ឌ
ជួបជុំគ្នាទៅវត្តយកកម្មគុផល
លេងល្បែងប្រជាប្រិយ

■ ■ ■ ■ ■

SovannKaory Sorn
age 8　Female
Cambodia（カンボジア）

お盆とお正月
お寺に集まってよいことをして
にんきのゲームをするよ

Scarecrows
Dancing with rice ears
In the rice fields

■ ■ ■ ■ ■

松嶋 朱理
Akari Matsushima
age 8　Female
Japan（日本）

かかしはね
田んぼのこめと
おどってる

Warm summer's night
Flowers bloom across the sky
Let's shout! Tamaya!

■ ■ ■ ■ ■

Edwina Du
age 13　Female
Australia（オーストラリア）

あたたかい夏の夜
空いっぱいに花がさく
大声で！「たまや！」

Mt. Shirakami
The sky clearing up
With a festival drum

■ ■ ■ ■ ■

清水 里乃伽
Rinoka Shimizu
age 10　Female
Japan（日本）

白神山
まつりだいこで
晴れわたる

年に一度だけ会える
一年中ソンクラーンだといいのに
タイの香水がにおうあたたかいハグ

Meeting once a year
I wish for a whole year of Songkran
Smelling Thai perfume with warm hugs

ปีหนึ่งได้พบหน้า
อยากให้มีสงกรานต์ทั้งปี
หอมน้ำอบ อุ่นกอด

■ ■ ■ ■ ■

Sunisa Watcharasawee
age12　Female　Thailand（タイ）

美しく浮かぶクラトン
線香とロウソクは楽しげに踊り
水の表面はステージのよう

Krathongs are floating beautifully
Incense sticks and candles are joyfully dancing
The water's surface is like a stage

กระทงลอยงามเด่น
ธูปเทียนเต้นรำเบิกบานใจ
ผืนน้ำเป็นเวที

■ ■ ■ ■ ■

Pannara Sripaiboon
age10 Female Thailand（タイ）

はしれ、水牛、はしれ
豊かな土のめぐみの日
たくさんたくさんとれた

Run carabao run
A day of fertile soil
Bountiful harvest

▪ ▪ ▪ ▪ ▪

Takbo kalabaw
Araw ng Pulang Lupa
Gapas biyaya

Mark Aron Daven Pereyra
age10　Male
Philippines（フィリピン）

風船のお祭り
さあ、一緒に行って空いっぱいに絵をかこう
自分の好きなようにね

Balloon Festival
Let's go and paint the whole sky
Make it yours always

▪ ▪ ▪ ▪ ▪

Maria Carmo Vaz Tome Frada
age11　Female
Portugal（ポルトガル）

稲刈(いねか)りをして
ガワイの日を祝う
感謝をささげて

Harvesting paddy
Celebrate Gawai Day
Signifying thanks

▪ ▪ ▪ ▪ ▪

Padi ditampi
Hari Gawai disambut
Tanda bersyukur

Ainur Basyirah Binti Abd Basid
age12　Female
Malaysia（マレーシア）

何百という提灯(ちょうちん)が
夜空に漂(ただよ)って
星になる

Hundreds of lanterns
Drifting across the night sky
Turning into stars

▪ ▪ ▪ ▪ ▪

Allison Farr
age13　Female
USA（米国／ハワイ）

木の下に
いろんな色あいのしきもの
秋

Under the trees
Rug of colorful shades
Autumn

■ ■ ■ ■ ■

Juria Vokovinsia
age11　Female　Croatia（クロアチア）

お祭りがはじまるよ
外をみると
いっせいに花がさいているよ

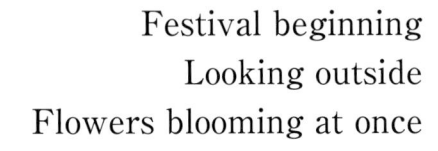

Festival beginning
Looking outside
Flowers blooming at once

La fête commence
Je vois dehors
Une fleurs qui écalt

■ ■ ■ ■ ■

Berrada Driss
age10　Male　Morocco（モロッコ）

Fall wind rising in August
The moon kicking out a floor cushion
Putting out the round abdomen

八月秋风起
月亮也会踢被子
露出圆肚皮

■ ■ ■ ■ ■

Yutong Qiu
age 8　Male
China（中国／上海）

八月に秋の風がふく
おふとんけとばしてお月さまは
丸いおなかをだしたよ

Round moon shining down
Lanterns hanging all around
Tea with mooncakes "Yum"

■ ■ ■ ■ ■

Lok Weng Tang
age 8　Female
Singapore（シンガポール）

丸いお月さまがみてる
提灯（ちょうちん）の光（ひかり）がたくさん
お茶と月餅（げっぺい）、「おいしい」

金色のくちびる
言葉飛び交う
秋

Golden lips
Words flying
Autumn

■ ■ ■ ■ ■

Lara Ana Kulenović
age11　Female
Croatia（クロアチア）

Boom boom
Floating on Lake Suwa
Fireworks in summer

■ ■ ■ ■ ■

木村 颯斗
Hayato Kimura
age 7　Male
Japan（日本）

ドードン
すわこにうかんだ
なつはなび

The full moon
Spotlights a long-nosed goblin
Dancing in the air

■ ■ ■ ■ ■

吉田 椋登
Mukuto Yoshida
age 9　Male
Japan（日本）

まん月の
スポットライト
てんぐまう

Round moon
When you crack it in two
It's the sun

圓圓像月亮
敲敲蛋殼敲敲敲
太陽掉出來

■ ■ ■ ■ ■

Yun-Yun Jhan
age 8　Female
Taiwan（台湾／台北）

月のようなまあるい卵
コツンと割れば
太陽だ

Fish swimming among lotus flowers
Waving ripples
A full moon night is so bright

鱼穿莲花丛
漾起一片水碧波
月儿十五明

■ ■ ■ ■ ■

Jiang Yang/Shijia Xu
age 15　Female
China（中国／上海）

蓮の花の間を泳ぐ魚
さざ波をたてて
満月の夜はこんなに明るい

Moon light
This is good enough
To dance with happiness

La lumière de la lune
Suffit pour donner
La joie de danser

Camille Lecolier
age 9 Female
Morocco（モロッコ）

月あかり
それだけでじゅうぶん
うれしくなって踊りだす

Autumn festival
Shouldering the portable shrine
Yo-Heave-ho!

秋祭り
おみこしかつぎ
よっこらしょ

高桑 百花
Momoka Takakuwa
age 9　Female
Japan（日本）

※点字（日本語）・点図作品／Braille work

目がさめて
いろいろな色の
秋

Awakened
In different colours
Autumn

■ ■ ■ ■ ■

Petra Vukovinski
age11　Female
Croatia（クロアチア）

お日さまのさいごの光が
冬じたくにいそがしい
おじさんたちの背中を照らす

The remaining sun gleaming
On hard-working men's backs
Getting ready for winter

■ ■ ■ ■ ■

Zak Jackson
age 9　Male
UK（英国）

3章 みんなでいわおう
Let's Celebrate Together!

知らない人とも
なかよしになれる
お祭りの日

Strangers they may be
Will become the closest friends
During feast day

Di kakilala
Naging magkaibigan
Dahil sa pista

Aaron John Fernandez
age12　Male　Philippines（フィリピン）

この特別な日に
みんな「いけ、いけ！」ってさけぶ
そして踊りだす

On this special day
All shouting "Go Go Ahead!"
And do your dancing

Sa tanging araw
Hala bira ang sigaw
Para magsayaw

■ ■ ■ ■ ■

Carlos Dominic Olegario
age15　Male　Philippines（フィリピン）

Firecrackers are banging loud
All brothers and sisters are delighted
Clapping hands together and celebrate

炮竹砰砰響
兄弟姊妹喜洋洋
熱鬧齊拍掌

■ ■ ■ ■ ■

Lok Yiu Yoyo Lee
age 9　Female
China（中国／香港）

爆竹バンバン
兄弟姉妹みんな嬉しくなって
一緒に手をたたいて祝います

数えきれないほどの提灯には
願いごとが書かれて
夜に浮かぶ

Thousands of lanterns
With wishes written on them
Floating in the night

Yee Lei Lee
age12　Female　Singapore（シンガポール）

願いごとはふわふわと
お日さまをおいかけながら
遠く地平線まではこばれる

Prayers drift away
Out to meet the Horizon
Pursuing the Sun

▪ ▪ ▪ ▪ ▪

Dakota Chun
age 9　Female　USA（米国／ハワイ）

ムルデカ独立記念日、万歳！
立派な国家の子どもたち
私は誇りに思います

Cheers of Merdeka!
Splendor of the nation's child
I am very proud

Sorak Merdeka
Semarak anak bangsa
Diriku bangga

■ ■ ■ ■ ■

Farah Nur Zulaika Binti Zainul Rijal
age12　Female　Malaysia（マレーシア）

Qingming Festival
Sweeping tombs and worshiping ancestors to remember one's origin
Joyful family reunion

清明時節
掃墓祭祖不忘典
全家樂團圓

■ ■ ■ ■ ■

Pei-Syuan Liao
age10　Female
Taiwan（台湾／高雄）

清明節
おはかをはいてご先祖様をうやまいわすれず
たのしい家族の集まり

It is Shrove Tuesday
Dad has got a new hairstyle
No it's a pancake

■ ■ ■ ■ ■

Bobby Lee
age10　Male
UK（英国）

告解火曜日だ
パパが髪型を新しくした
と思ったらパンケーキがのっていた

At the Japanese Festival
We watch dances
And catch many fish

■ ■ ■ ■ ■

Gavin Bejerana
age10　Male
USA（米国／グアム）

日本祭で
踊りをみて
金魚をたくさんつかまえた

Pippi's festival
We were dancing in line
It was veeery looong

Pikin festival
Igrali smo se vlakec
Bil je zelooo dooolg

Vid Satler
age11　Male　Slovenia（スロベニア）

ピッピのお祭り
ぼくたちは一列になって踊る
すごーくながーくなって

子どもたちは走って遊ぶ
いたる所に様々な色が
そしてみんなつながって

Kids run and have fun
Where colors are everywhere
And everyone bonds

▪ ▪ ▪ ▪ ▪

Alvaro Rivas
age13　Male　USA（米国本土）

花火と万国旗
たき火、ランタン、歌
みんなとっても素晴らしい

Fireworks and bunting
Bonfires, lanterns and singing
All is so stunning

■ ■ ■ ■ ■

Hannah Slack
age12 Female
Switzerland（スイス）

新年のお祭りだ
みんな楽しんでいる
私は身障(しんしょう)者(しゃ)の妹の世話をしなくちゃ

It's the New Year Festival
Everyone is enjoying themselves
I got to look after my disabled sister

เทศกาลปีใหม่
ทุกคนเที่ยวสนุกสนาน
ฉันเลี้ยงน้องพิการ

■ ■ ■ ■ ■

Suchanya Suwan
age12　Female
Thailand（タイ）

Infinite canvas
Chrysanthemums bursting with
Color and power

■ ■ ■ ■ ■

Arianna Krischenbaum
age13　Female
USA（米国／ハワイ）

無限のキャンヴァス
はちきれんばかりに
菊の色と力

お互いの手をさしのべて
お互いに目を合わせよう
世界はひとつになる

Add each other's hand
And each other's glance
The world becomes one

손길 하나
눈길 하나 더하여
하나된 세계

Hayoung Jeon
age14　Female　Korea（韓国）

こころが踊る
断食明けのお祭りの間じゅう
みんなのために

My heart is cheerful
During Eid festival
For everyone

Hati ceria
Selamat Hari Raya
Untuk semua

■■■■■

Leong Ka Hei
age11　Female
Malaysia（マレーシア）

壮麗な祝典
ああ！　音楽はほんとうにやさしく
人々はまじり合う

Grand Celebration
The music, oh so gentle
People are mingling

Marangyang piging
Musika ay magiliw
Tao'y kasaliw

■■■■■

Giselle Ann Melgar
age15　Female
Philippines（フィリピン）

お空に満月
灯った提灯は絵みたいにきれい
月餅を食べながら一緒におしゃべり

Full moon hanging in the sky
Lighted lanterns are as beautiful as paintings
Having mooncakes and chatting together

圓月天上掛
點起燈籠美如畫
吃餅齊共話

Yan Ning Charis Law
age11　Female
China（中国／香港）

ありさんは
おまつりしても
ちいさいね

Ants are small
Aren't they?
Even at their festival

■ ■ ■ ■ ■

川島 結
Yui Kawashima
age 7　Female
Japan（日本）

ドドルがでてきた
レマン、ケトゥパットに肉料理のレンダン
おいしそうでわくわくしちゃう

Dodol has been served
Lemang, Ketupat, Rendang
It elates my heart

Dodol terhidang
Lemang, Ketupat, Rendang
Hatiku girang

・・・・・

Sofea Arisya Binti Muhammad Shaifuddin
age10　Female
Malaysia（マレーシア）

がんばれと
うちわをふるよ
よーいやさぁ

**Do your best!
Waving round fans
Hurrah! Hurrah!**

・・・・・

長谷川 高広
Takahiro Hasegawa
age 11　Male
Japan（日本）

Multiple ethnics
Celebrating together
Cheerful and happy

Pelbagai Kaum
Perayaan bersama
Riang gembira

▪▪▪▪▪

Muhammad Aiman Bin Mahadzir
age12
Malaysia（マレーシア）

多民族
みんなでお祝い
楽しいな

夏祭り
みんなのえがおが
たくさんだ

Summer festival
Everybody smiling
A lot of people

▪▪▪▪▪

矢野 一真
Kazuma Yano
age10　Male
Taiwan（台湾／台北）

Midnight arrives, CRASH！
Streamers through the night sky, BOOM！
Happy New Year, BANG！

▪▪▪▪▪

Scott McClain
age14　Male
USA（米国／ハワイ）

午前零時(れい)だ、ガシャン！
夜空をわたる光のすじ、ドーン！
新年おめでとう、バン！

暗闇(くらやみ)に提灯(ちょうちん)
星空の下で会う
どの家も笑い声でいっぱい

Lanterns in the dark
We all meet under the stars
All homes full of laughter

▪▪▪▪▪

Yin Ching Chang
age10　Female
China（中国／香港）

80

世界中で
虹(にじ)の山車(だし)が通りにあふれる
お祭りにいらっしゃい

All over the world
The rainbow floats fill the streets
Join the festival

■ ■ ■ ■ ■

Amy Honeyman
age10　Female
Australia（オーストラリア）

おわりに

二〇一一年三月十一日、未曾有の大震災が東日本を襲い、数多くの尊い命が失われました。この東日本大震災の被害は甚大なものでしたが、ただちに世界中から我が国に対して温かい支援が寄せられたことは、記憶に新しいと思います。

先日、作家・村上春樹さんの「国際交流基金賞」の授賞式に参加する機会をいただきました。残念ながら、ご本人は、海外で生活をし仕事をしているために、当日の式典には参加できませんでしたが、彼の寄せたスピーチに次のくだりがあります。

「現実の我々の世界には地理的な国境があります。残念ながら、というべきかどうかはわかりませんが、とにかくそれは存在します。そしてそれは時として摩擦を生み、政治問題を引き起こします。文化の世界にもちろん国境はあります。でも地理上の国境とは違い、心を定めさえすれば、私たちにはそれを易々とまたぎ超えることができます。言葉が違い生活様式が異なっても、物語という心のあり方を等価交換的に共有することができます。」

残念ながら、地球上ではいまだ紛争が絶えません。しかしながら、時間はかかるかもしれませんが、私たちはお互いに理解しあうことにより、村上さんがおっしゃる「文化の国境」を越えることができると確信しています。冒頭の世界各国からの支援も、まさに私たちの心が国境を越えようとしていることの現れではないでしょうか。このように、お互いに危機を乗り越え、協力して繁栄と幸福を追求することができる国際社会の実現のため、この「世界こどもハイクコンテスト」も微力ながら一役買いたいと願いつつ、コンテストの運営に取り組んでいるところです。

最後に、一九九〇年に始まったこのコンテストも、今回で十二回目を迎えました。このコンテストは、日本のみならず世界各国の教育機関の皆様、選考にご協力いただいた日本学生俳句協会や世界各国の審査員の皆様、日本航空海外支店、国際俳句交流協会、ブロンズ新社など、多くの関係者のご協力のもと実施してまいりました。この場をお借りして、心より御礼を申し上げます。

財団法人　日航財団
常務理事　中川　浩昌

＊「第十三回世界こどもハイクコンテスト」は、二〇一三年、「夢」をテーマに開催する予定です。世界中の子どもたちからの作品をお待ちしています。詳細は日航財団ウェブサイト（http://www.jal-foundation.or.jp）をご参照下さい。

On March 11, 2011, an earthquake of unprecedented scale hit the eastern part of Japan and claimed an enormous number of precious lives. While the Great East Japan Earthquake brought vast devastation, the warm support extended to Japan from all over the world is still fresh in our minds.

The other day, I had an opportunity to attend the commendation ceremony of "The Japan Foundation Awards" for author Haruki Murakami. Unfortunately, Mr. Murakami was not present at the ceremony as he currently lives and works overseas, so he sent a written message instead. One passage stuck in my mind: "In this real world of ours, there exist geographical borders. I don't know whether or not I should add 'unfortunately' to this statement, but in any case, these borders between nations do exist. At times, they give rise to friction and to political problems. In the world of culture, too, there exist borders. But unlike geographical borders, these borders between cultures can be crossed quite easily by us if only we make up our minds to cross them. Though language and lifestyle may differ from one culture to the next, it is possible for us to share each other's stories across cultures on an absolutely equal footing." (excerpt from the Japan Foundation website)

Regrettably, conflicts never seem to cease on this planet. But I firmly believe that through mutual understanding, we can overcome these cultural borders, although it may take time. The support that Japan received from all over the world right after the disaster was strong testimony to people's efforts to overcome the barriers of the mind. We would like to build an international community where we can overcome crises and pursue prosperity and happiness together. We have been hosting the "World Children's Haiku Contest" with the sincere hope that the contest may play a small but meaningful part toward that goal.

The "World Children's Haiku Contest" started in 1990 and we just concluded its 12th session. The contest has been made possible through cooperation and support from various individuals, firms and organizations, including educational institutions in Japan as well as in many other countries, judges from Japan Student Haiku Association and also many individual judges overseas, Japan Airlines' overseas branches, Haiku International Association, Bronze Shinsha and many others. We wish to extend our heartfelt gratitude to all concerned.

Hiromasa Nakagawa
Managing Director
JAL Foundation

The 13th "World Children's Haiku Contest" will be held in 2013 under the theme of "Dreams." We look forward to seeing haiku from children all over the world. For more details, please visit the JAL Foundation website. (http://www.jal-foundation.or.jp)

Epilogue

Constanca Duarte 40
Maria Carmo Vaz Tome Frada 54

Singapore シンガポール

Hui Shern Lee　表紙/Front Cover
Xing Yuan Tan 8
Rytasha Passion Raj 18
Wen Siew Shanna Lim 32
Zhi-Xin Isaiah Lai 34
Lok Weng Tang 57
Yee Lei Lee 66

Slovenia スロベニア

Jan Tunanovič 37
Jan Eller 42
Marko Lumbar 43
Sara Ferlež 45
Vid Satler 70

Switzerland スイス

Hannah Slack 72

Taiwan 台湾(台北・高雄)

Wei-Hao Huang　裏表紙/Back Cover
Wen-Shin Lu 9
Yu-Chia Hu 20
Jing-Han Liao 26
Chia-Yu Hsieh 31
Chia-Ning Chuang 47
Chin-Ting Hsu 49
Ya-Tze Wu 49
Yun-Yun Jhan 59
Pei-Syuan Liao 69
Kazuma Yano 80

Thailand タイ

Ornrampha Boonsomchue 23
Chetsinee Chaikhun 35
Orathai Yimyoung 36
Thitirat Saeoung 39
Chalita Kaeokoon 41
Sunisa Watcharasawee 52
Pannara Sripaiboon 53
Suchanya Suwan 73

Turkey トルコ

Talin Harun 33

UK 英国

Alex Gibbs 7
Owen Boyle 19
Esme Winterbotham 25
Robbie Easton 25
Matthew Burton 28
Jessica Williams 35
Zak Jackson 62
Bobby Lee 69

USA 米国(米国本土・ハワイ・グアム)

Christine Littrice 6
Noah Hirashima 10
Zelda Cole 12
Megan Lauw 13
Isabella Joy Teramae 15
Aleah Carino 33
Sara Tamadon 33
Simpkins Zena 36
Ella Pobre 46
Allison Farr 54
Dakota Chun 67
Gavin Bejerana 69
Alvaro Rivas 71
Arianna Krischenbaum 73
Scott McClain 80

Vietnam ベトナム

Lam Thu Huynh Tran 39

INDEX

Australia オーストラリア
Sandra Zelic　36
Lilian Shepherd　43
Edwina Du　51
Amy Honeyman　81

Cambodia カンボジア
SovannKaory Sorn　51

Canada カナダ
Elli Collins　11

China 中国（上海・香港）
Xuyang Zhu　14
Yueming Xu　16
Yunran Tang　24
Yan Yan Carol Chang　29
Mila Zou　30
Xiangheng Chen　35
Long Yat Chow　43
Hei Long Ma　48
Wan Chun Ashley Wong　49
Yutong Qiu　57
Jiang Yang/Shijia Xu　59
Lok Yiu Yoyo Lee　65
Yan Ning Charis Law　76
Yin Ching Chang　80

Croatia クロアチア
Juria Vokovinsia　55
Lara Ana Kulenović　58
Petra Vukovinski　62

France フランス
Sixtine Demourgues　17
Mayu Hirata　38
Carla Stanichi　44

Japan 日本
Mizuka Shinagawa　11
Kanami Jinba　25
Ryunosuke Abe　27
Daijiro Sanenobu　30
Yuki Miki　30
Madoka Niki　39
Kanae Murakami　50
Akari Matsushima　51
Rinoka Shimizu　51
Hayato Kimura　59
Mukuto Yoshida　59
Momoka Takakuwa　61
Yui Kawashima　77
Takahiro Hasegawa　79

Korea 韓国
Yejin Lee　35
Minju Im　39
Hayoung Jeon　74

Malaysia マレーシア
Ainur Basyirah Binti Abd Basid　54
Farah Nur Zulaika Binti Zainul Rijal　68
Leong Ka Hei　75
Sofea Arisya Binti Muhammad Shaifuddin　78
Muhammad Aiman Bin Mahadzir　80

Morocco モロッコ
Inès Hersan　5
Lucie Bellegarde　28
Berrada Driss　56
Camille Lecolier　60

Philippines フィリピン
Andrea Louise Matulac　11
Shanaia Jane Bual　11
Gabriel Evan Blanco　22
Mark Aron Daven Pereyra　54
Aaron John Fernandez　63
Carlos Dominic Olegario　64
Giselle Ann Melgar　75

Portugal ポルトガル
Ara Magarida Brandao　21
Mykola Yashchok　28

地球歳時記
おまつりのうた
Impressions of Festivals

2013年2月25日 初版第1刷発行

編 者　日航財団

装丁者　籾山真之(snug.)
発行者　若月眞知子
発行所　ブロンズ新社
　　　　東京都渋谷区神宮前6-31-15-3B
　　　　03-3498-3272
　　　　http://www.bronze.co.jp/

印　刷　吉原印刷
製　本　大村製本

©2013 JAL FOUNDATION
ISBN978-4-89309-563-3 C8076

本書に掲載されている、全ての文章及び画像等の無断転用を禁じます。

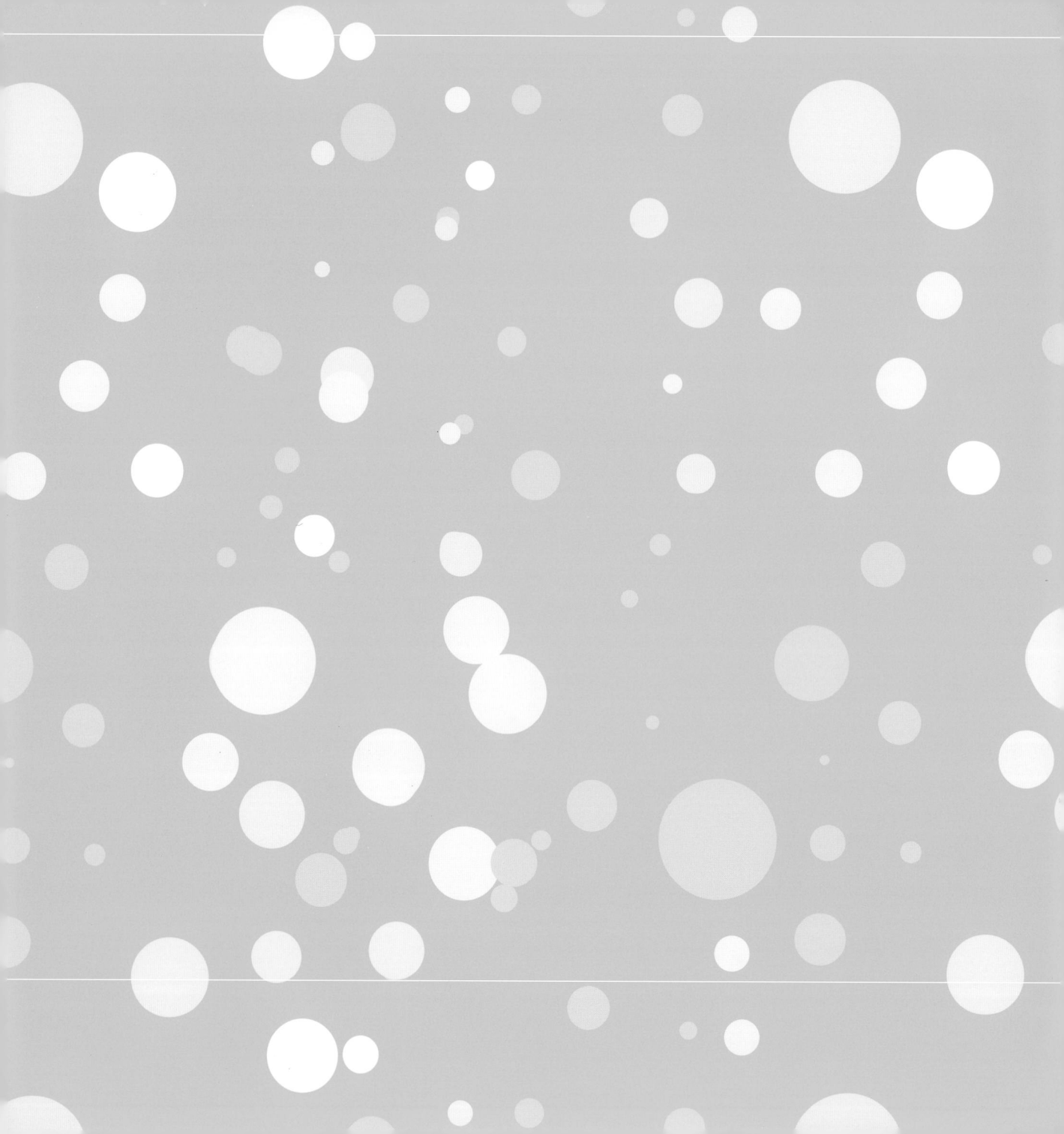